Is America and the World Headed for Destruction?

Dr. Robbi Warren

For more information, write:
Robbi Warren International Ministries,
PO Box 724
Upper Marlboro, MD 20773.
(800) 478-4225.
rwministry@netscape.net

ISBN (paperback)
ISBN (hardcover)

Printed in the United States of America

Dedication

This book is dedicated to the memory of my paternal grandparents, Lawrence and Dorothy Warren, who lovingly raised me from the age of five months and formally adopted me around the age of eleven or twelve. Their guidance instilled in me a deep reverence for the Lord. I also honor my biological parents, William Sr. and Mary Francis Warren (R.I.P.), who brought me into this world. I am deeply grateful to my great-grandparents, Frank and Mamie McClain (R.I.P.). To my siblings William Jr. (R.I.P.), Michael, Joe Frank, Greg, Anthony, and Demetrius and my sisters, Doris, Karen, Phyllis, and Classy, as well as the rest of my family, I extend my heartfelt appreciation. I also dedicate this work to those who have blessed me both spiritually and naturally throughout this journey: my pastors, spiritual mothers, and fathers, including Pastor Willie and Dorothy Perkins, Pastor James Kilgore, Mother Narvie Green, Bishop Willie Smith, Pastor Winnie Gilliam,

Bishop James Nelson Sr., Bishop James Tyson, Bishop Chandler D. Owens, Bishop George McKinney, my sister T. Carter, my brother Jack, Pastor Terry Russell, and Pastor Marlon Baylor. I am grateful to all the pastors who have opened their churches to allow me to minister in the Holy Spirit. Special thanks to my music producers, Jonathan Dubose Jr., and my mentor, Pastor Andrae Crouch (R.I.P.), as well as Terry, Greg, and my WATC family; Kevin and my family; The Word Network; and my television production colleague, Fred Windham (R.I.P.). I am profoundly thankful to Dr. Neal F. Hambright for his administrative expertise and steadfast support throughout this project. Your labor is truly not in vain. I also thank Mark at 48 Hour Books for his valuable insight.

Above all, I dedicate this work to my Lord and Savior, Jesus Christ. To God be the glory.

Disclaimer

After reading this book, I pray that the message does not get lost in the climate of politics or the bias of one side against the other. As a born-again believer, I'm looking at things from a biblical and spiritual perspective, not a biased one. This book is not about bashing any leader, spiritual or natural. There are spirits and a system that deals with the Antichrist, the man of sin. But some of the things that we are exposed to, we must realize, are part of God's plan.

And it's not only the leader of the free world, but also others who seem to be under the influence of that spirit. This includes some church leaders, secular leaders, and people in general. Keep in mind that Satan and his demons know this. Therefore, they also know that there are times and that mankind is short. In these last days, the enemy's primary assignment is to deceive the world.

The great deceiver, Satan, is always looking for people he can use as tools to carry out his deceptive plans. Always remember, it is appointed unto man once to die, but after death comes the judgment. That means ending up in heaven or hell the lake of fire, as we believers believe. No matter what our political affiliations are or the color of our skin, we have a date with judgment. Let me repeat this: any of us can become a tool of Satan. The devil and his demons are looking for a physical body to carry out their plans.

Now you understand what the intention of this book is all about.

Judge it for yourself!

Table of Contents

Chapter 1

What Is Bible Prophecy?

Let me explain the difference between Prophecy and Prophesy. Prophecy is communicating a divine message from God to humanity, often through a Prophet, Prophetess, or those who claim to hear from God directly. This message can predict future events or a spiritual truth intended to guide and prepare people via the Holy Spirit.

These messages are given to warn and to give insights into God's plan. The ultimate destination of those who are Born Again Believers and those who are not when Jesus Christ returns as the Messiah, according to Christianity, and the future of nations mentioned in the Christian Bible. Prophetic passages are found throughout the Bible, in Daniel, Ezekiel, Matthew, and Revelation, and are often associated with end-time prophecy.

Prophecy should be understood as divine communication:

Prophecy is fundamentally a message from God delivered to a human recipient, called a Prophet, Prophetess, or anyone claiming to be a Spokesperson for God.

Do you know the purpose of Bible Prophecy? Let me attempt to explain.

Prophecy can serve various purposes, including:

- **Foretelling the Future:** This includes specific predictions of events, the coming of a Messiah, and fulfilling God's promises.

- **Spiritual Truth:** Prophecies can offer interpretations and a deeper understanding of God's will and moral and spiritual principles, guiding those who have a hunger for God.

Prophecy offers insight and a framework for understanding world events, helping people prepare for future outcomes and God's plan. Now, let's examine different types of prophecy. Some prophecies are conditional, meaning their fulfillment depends on how people or nations respond.

Focus on God's Plan: End-time prophecies often highlight the broader course of history, culminating in Jesus Christ's return and the establishment of God's kingdom.

Gives biblical insight and authority:

Believers see biblical prophecy as an accurate reflection of God's communication, intended to offer comfort, encourage those to live righteous and holy lives, and protect against deception.

Examples of prophecy:

- The death, burial, and resurrection of our Lord and Savior Jesus Christ

- The future of the nation of Israel

- Global political and natural events in the "last days"

- The destination of all human beings is to establish a Messianic Kingdom.

We must clearly understand that prophecy is the divine message from God, while prophesy is the act of delivering or proclaiming that message.

Think of "prophecy" as a message coming directly from God, and " prophesy " as a person delivering the Word like a direct download from the Spirit.

Prophecy Definition: A prediction, a divinely inspired utterance, or knowledge of the future, often from a divine source.

Purpose: To carry divine messages, warn, give hope, or proclaim truth from a deity.

This is what true men and women of Jesus Christ should be doing prophesying the prophecy already established biblically.

Examples:
As you study the prophecies of Nostradamus, consider his subjects concerning time and the end of the world as we know it.

Prophesy Definition: To predict the future, usually with divine inspiration, or to act as a spokesman for God. But it could also be for Satan, as well.

Purpose: The action of delivering divine communication, which can serve to edify, exhort, and comfort believers.

Examples:

"A prophet/prophetess or anyone must be careful not to prophesy falsely."
As in saying the Lord or the Holy Ghost told me this or that.

Now, even though God uses people, so does Satan. Why don't people know this? Maybe because they haven't been taught. We should be prophesying the prophecies, and there are many of them recorded in the Bible, including warnings that "many false prophets shall rise and deceive many" Matthew 24:11. So, what are the characteristics of those considered false prophets?

1. They present themselves as righteous: They may appear to be religious leaders, acting as ministers of God.

2. They are consumed by pride, filled with self-importance and self-admiration, leaving no space in their hearts for Jesus Christ."

There are those who claim to speak on behalf of God and the Holy Ghost use words that appeal only to the flesh for self-gratification and validation. This is very serious, and people need to know.

Chapter 2

The Importance of Bible Prophecy

In this hour, we need to examine biblical applications, calls for repentance, and warnings: Prophecy provides hope and calls people to repentance, warning them of the consequences of sin and the need to return to God. It emphasizes the importance of discerning spirits. The existence of false prophets is a significant warning in the Bible, highlighting the need to examine what is contrary to Scripture to distinguish true messengers from false ones.

Focuses on God's Ultimate Victory:
Our primary focus of biblical prophecy should be the Second Coming of Christ. This future event offers freedom from sin and provides believers with a clear focus for their lives. Additionally, we must recognize that prophecy is crucial in giving instruction and guidance. This was mainly part of the old covenant concerning Israel and the men and women of God, such as David, Samuel, Elisha, Elijah, Isaiah, Jeremiah, and many others.

We find both the minor and major prophets when we examine these individuals. Throughout the scriptures, even Jeremiah 29:8-9 shows this. Jeremiah, known as the weeping prophet, was sent by God to speak to the Kings, Priest, and the people's prophets because of their rebellion against God while in bondage.

God's prophets were isolated from the people, the king, and the priest. When you think about the school of the prophets, which is referenced in the scriptures, the school of the prophets was men whom God set aside, and they had teachers who taught them what it meant to be consecrated and dedicated to the Lord.

So, they could hear from God and not man. That's why if you go to the book of Jeremiah, you can read where Jeremiah said, "For thus saith the LORD of hosts, the God of Israel; Let not your prophets and your diviners, that be in the midst of you, deceive you, neither hearken to your dreams which ye cause to be dreamed. For they prophesy falsely unto you in my name: I have not sent them, saith the LORD." Jeremiah 29:8-9 (KJV). Now we see the difference between God's and the people's prophets. The people's prophets spoke what they wanted to hear.

In the book of Isaiah 30:10, "which say to the seers, see not; and to the prophets, prophesy not unto us right things, speak unto us smooth things, prophesy deceits:" While in prison, Isaiah still spoke what thus said the Lord. The prophets of God were not welcome. The prophets of God were persecuted.

When they came to the region, the king, the priest, their prophets, and people did not want to accept the prophets of God because the word they would speak was not favorable to the flesh. Most of the prophets of God were killed. They were totally opposed to the people's prophets. Think about it for a second. I want people reading this to understand we have the same problem today. But when we go to the new covenant, after the death, burial, and resurrection of our Lord and Savior Jesus Christ, and we will talk about it a little later, the veil was ripped.

God was able to speak to His people after they received His Spirit. This is what the conflict is today. We don't need men or women speaking for God 24/7; this is the deception. I don't want to discuss this subject much longer because I will revisit it as you move on to other chapters and reiterate.

Chapter 3

Three Things to Watch: Church, Governments/World Events, and the Weather

Let's look at the church according Bible prophecy we can see it mentioned as well in the scriptures discussing prophecy and foreshadowing. The Church is built on Christ the apostles at Pentecost, and its future is as a faithful people waiting for Christ's return, either by the rapture before the tribulation or death witnessing the Second Coming. The Book of Revelation uses symbols to show the church as a faithful woman and mentions the church in the context of the end times and Christ's return.

Establishment in Jerusalem:

Isaiah prophesied that the Lord's house would be built on the highest mountains, with the law spreading from Zion and the word of the Lord coming from Jerusalem. This prophecy came true at Pentecost, when the Holy Spirit was poured out and the Church started in Jerusalem.

Foundation of Christ:
Isaiah's prophecy of a "precious cornerstone" in Zion (Jerusalem) is expanded by Paul in Ephesians, who identifies Christ as the chief cornerstone and the household of God as built upon the apostles and prophets.

Between Jesus Christ's first and second comings started the Church Age, a time when Jesus established His church and guaranteed that the forces of evil would not overcome it.

Remaining Steadfast in Times of Chaos:
As the end times approach, the church is portrayed as a community of faithful people who hold tight to God's teachings and stand out as holy in a world marked by evil. My research also provides insights into the early Church Fathers and the development of various reformations and beliefs about Jesus Christ and churches.

Indeed, there are numerous churches and various beliefs tied to Christianity. Therefore, the part Christianity plays in what some refer to as the last days or end times will differ. The question is: How do we explain the church and its role in Bible prophecy for the last days? That's a great question, and it sparks some lively debates. However, I think the core of Christianity and churches is founded on faith and personal experiences.

At its core, the Church is a gathering place where people unite to worship God and Jesus Christ. Even those there are those who don't believe in the Church or Jesus Christ as the Messiah it doesn't change his authority and His Kingship. Jesus says in Matthew 16:18, "And I say also unto thee, that thou art Peter, and upon this rock I will build my church; and the gates of hell shall not prevail against it."

This verse comes after Peter confesses Jesus as the Christ, and Jesus confirms that confession and promises to build His church on the "rock" of that truth. In a widely used translation (English Standard Version), the verse reads: "And I tell you, you are Peter, and on this rock, I will build my church, and the gates of hell shall not prevail against it." What does "This Rock" Symbolize? While some interpret "this rock" as Peter himself, the common understanding is that Jesus refers to Peter's confession that Jesus is the Christ, the Son of the living God.

Therefore, the church is built on the fundamental truth of who Christ is, not on Peter. What a promise for those born-again believers! We can also look back at the church's long history, which has faced persecution, and those who represent this body of believers. The Body of Christ often refers to the people who make up this body. According to prophecy, some followers of Christ will face persecution, suffering, and even death for representing Jesus on earth.

We should remember that, from the very beginning, Jesus's purpose was to destroy Satan's works. After His death, burial, resurrection, and the Holy Spirit's outpouring on Pentecost, He has given us the power to continue His mission. When we think about the church, there are three signs we need to watch for in these last days. We've already discussed the church. Now, let's look at the government and world events around us.

We must consider that the Christian Bible encourages us to think beyond what we see and feel in the world we live in or were born into. I believe it is a prophetic book. Some may not believe in it that's their choice. Some will not even accept it. Even within religious groups not only in Christianity but also in Judaism, Islam, and Hinduism. I want to share a few things concerning the government and the world that were so prophetically mentioned in the Christian Bible.

Hear me out: Many religious readers and commentators see links between government, world events, and biblical prophecy. This viewpoint is often up for debate, with many interpretations coming from various theological approaches and denominations. Certain books and passages in the Bible, like Daniel and Revelation, contain visions that some would call prophetic, relating to worldly governments and events at the end of time. These events aren't limited to the United States or Israel.

They're not isolated to our Christian leaders or even Christian scholars. I often reference two types of scholars: Christian scholars, and Bible scholars. The difference between the two is one is a Christian, and the other is not. Biblical prophecies about government and world events often mention the idea of a one-world government.

This means superpowers will align themselves to create a coalition like the United Nations or the League of Nations. But in the biblical text, we believe this will happen in the future: a powerful, centralized global authority that will govern all nations a one-world government. Many believe that in the Book of Revelation, chapter 13, and other passages, the beast is given authority over every tribe, people, tongue, and nation (Revelation 13:7).

The prophet Daniel also wrote about this, as seen in the book of Daniel. We know about Shadrach, Meshach, Abednego, and Daniel from chapter 1, where God placed them in positions after their enslavement. They were taught the language and learning of the Chaldeans, but the Hebrew boys refused to bow to idols. It wasn't just the three of them; Daniel was included. They promised their God not to eat food offered to idols. These young men stood their ground when it came to their faith in Jehovah, skilled in science, and intelligent. Daniel 1:4

If you read Daniel 1, you can see God's sovereign hand at work—how He places people in certain positions to represent him. Consider this for a moment. Even when we look at Shadrach, Meshach, and Abednego, who were ordered to bow down, they all found favor in God's eyes. Daniel stood with the Hebrew boys, and they all knew their mission was to honor Jehovah. They were willing to die rather than compromise their faith and refused to bow to the king's gods when commanded. The king issued a decree to pray and bow, but they stood firm in their commitment to God.

In short, we see individuals who remained strong in adversity. When we summarize and paraphrase events in the book of Daniel, a prophetic book, some accounts describe past prophecies. Prophecy often focuses on the past, present, and future. The books of Daniel and Revelation, along with passages like Matthew 24 (where Jesus discusses the end times), provide insight into these times.

Several world events have already occurred, including the coming of the Messiah, Israel's establishment as a nation, and the founding of a kingdom. In the New Covenant, Jesus prayed, "Thy kingdom come, thy will be done on earth as it is in heaven." You can also find this in John 14, where Jesus reassures us, "Let not your heart be troubled." As you can see, He is giving the believer comfort. That same chapter also prophetically foretells the outpouring of the Holy Spirit. Jesus told His disciples, "Greater works than these shall ye do." It's incredible how the scriptures give us a glimpse into what we're experiencing today.

The outpouring of the Holy Spirit occurred on the Feast of Pentecost and had a global impact. Shadrach, Meshach, and Abednego refused to bow down. They didn't argue with the king. Daniel didn't argue either; he asked the prince of the eunuchs not to defile him with the king's food and wine, which had been offered to idols.

The eunuchs were worried because they didn't want the king to see the Hebrew boys looking starved or unhealthy. But they were just as healthy as those who gave in. God allowed them to be bound in Babylon (see Daniel 1). When they were thrown into the fiery furnace for not bowing to the idol, notice what happened: the king leaped to his feet and exclaimed, "Didn't we throw three men into the fire? But here are four, and the fourth looks like the Son of God." The king ordered them out of the fire, and their clothes were unharmed, showing no smell of smoke. The men who had thrown them in were consumed. This demonstrates the sustaining power of God when it comes to His servants.

They were willing to die, but God rescued them. King Nebuchadnezzar declared that no god could match this and gave them special treatment. Despite shifting from one government to another, these young men embodied the kingdom of God in a time when the government didn't acknowledge Jehovah.

Later, Daniel was promoted to lead all the presidents and administrators because of his ability to interpret the king's dream. Your gifts will lead to your promotion, even in times of wickedness. When Daniel was caught praying and defying the king's decree, he didn't try to change the king but let his light shine. Despite being thrown into the lions' den, Daniel kept praying.

The king, worried about him, fasted for his sake. Daniel prayed to God, whom the king didn't know. When Daniel was finally delivered, God heard his prayer, but a demonic force possibly the prince of Persia delayed the answer. Angels intervened and told Daniel, "We heard your prayer 21 days ago, but a demonic force held up the answer." Although they couldn't stop his prayer, they hindered the answer.

As we enter this unprecedented time, which I believe marks the end times, an apostate church is already in place, but we're focusing on the government and the world now. When you examine Daniel's prophecies, the beast represents earthly powers and empires. By studying the histories of these empires, you can gain a deeper understanding and see the bigger picture.

Some might say, "I don't buy into any of this." That's your choice. But I encourage you to consider the bigger picture. Take your time, and you'll see what I'm getting at. There are multiple perspectives and interpretations, like in Daniel 7 and Daniel 9. These passages hint at how Satan (Antichrist) will try to wear out the saints. Many scholars and theologians believe these chapters are part of a larger event.

Some believe that Trump being a part of the agreement with the Abraham Accords was a sign associated with the Antichrist in biblical prophecy. If you read Daniel 7:9, you will better understand what I am conveying (symbolism). Others might not understand the symbols and creatures mentioned. Some point out that the United States isn't explicitly mentioned in the Bible prophecy, but many nations aren't mentioned because they haven't yet been formed. These are called providential nations with characteristics that fit Bible prophecy and could become part of the one-world government.

Although the Bible doesn't directly reference a "one-world government," we can observe how nations form alliances. You can draw your own conclusions. What does it mean when the leader of the United States, one of the world's most influential countries, aligns with Russia? Many people believe other nations will join forces and eventually descend from the north to attack Israel.

It's interesting to note that if these places weren't mentioned in the Bible, we wouldn't have references to ancient Persia (Iran), Babylon (Iraq), Damascus, Syria, and others. Some people may not realize that Iran is the modern equivalent of ancient Persia, and Iraq is the modern equivalent of ancient Babylon. Revelation 13 and other passages highlight the inability to buy or sell without the mark of the beast, the number of the beast (666), and the Antichrist.

We're witnessing world events aligning wars and rumors of wars, alliances between Russia, China, North Korea, and Middle Eastern nations opposed to Israel. The United States is one of Israel's strongest allies. Israel was established as a nation in 1948. We're seeing European countries, including Germany, backing Ukraine against Russia. Do you see what I see? Are you hearing what I'm hearing?

According to the Bible, many scholars and theologians believe this is a prophecy, and we should be prepared for what's to come. Make up your own mind. Look at world events and governments and see how they compare. How do government and world events tie into Bible prophecy? I hope you're reading with an open mind. I can provide many relevant scriptures, but some may argue that they don't fit or are misinterpreted. That's your call. Instead, why not compare the scriptures for yourself? Grab your Bible and look at Daniel 7:25.

Read the whole chapter and use resources like Google to help you understand the symbols. Then, check out Revelation 13. Just read and see what stands out to you. I know you might not understand the symbols of the four beasts. Remarkably, there are four beasts in Daniel and four in Revelation. If I remember correctly, even the four horsemen are mentioned. Please learn this for yourself and don't rely only on me and others.

Watch the church, watch the government, and watch the world. Do your own research and study. I see various perspectives as I explore other information recorded online through Google, AI searches, commentaries, and different schools of thought. Most use the same Bible, but their approach to Bible prophecy eschatology varies across Christian denominations. Many people call this futurism.

The futurist perspective believes that most of the Book of Revelation and other end-time prophecies will still be fulfilled and occur just before Jesus Christ's return. It's hard to accuse people of plagiarism because few schools of thought on Bible prophecy exist. There are three main views on this topic: pre-tribulation, mid-tribulation, and post-tribulation. These views are related to Bible prophecy.

Some people believe Jesus will return before the tribulation period (pre-trib), while others think He'll return in the middle of it (mid-trib), and still others believe He'll come after the great tribulation (post-trib). Mid-trib believers often claim they'll experience tribulation, but not the great tribulation, citing verses that say God hasn't appointed us to His wrath. However, the Bible mentions two types of wrath: God's wrath and Satan's wrath. Our understanding of the world, the government, and global events is still evolving.

Additionally, some preterists believe that the first century AD fulfilled many, if not all, of the prophecies in Daniel and Revelation, and they claim that these prophecies no longer apply to us today. You can explore this perspective as well. Some people see Revelation and other prophetic books, like Daniel, as symbolic stories representing the spiritual struggle between good and evil, rather than actual historical events. In this view, it's a battle between good and evil, not a record of specific events.

Some people, known as historicists, see biblical prophecy as a preview of the entire history of the Christian church, from the first century until the Second Coming. We're talking about the Christian church and the Bible, which many consider the breath and word of God. Others believe it's humanity's interpretation of God, based on their experiences. We'll leave that debate for another time.

Take it all in for yourself or pray and ask the Lord to speak to your heart. I want to caution against jumping to conclusions. Many theologians advise against directly linking current events to biblical prophecy. The Bible warns against trying to predict God's timing (Mark 13:32). I'm not saying I have it all figured out; I'm just sharing information and encouraging you to do your comparative study. Ultimately, it comes down to whether you believe in prophecy or not.

Some scholars argue that biblical prophecy wasn't meant to be a secret code for future headlines. However, many people accepted that the prophecies pointed to the future because they didn't live during those times. It's incredible how the Bible predicts that knowledge will grow. The King James Version was likely among the first Western translations to help Christians understand the original texts.

Since the Bible was written in Hebrew and Greek, we need translations and transliterations to make it accessible. These advancements are fascinating. As I mentioned earlier, go ahead with your comparative study. While many prophecies refer to the future, they can be challenging to decipher without context. It wasn't until the 19th and 20th centuries that people started interpreting them in a way that matched the written text, and they began to witness things coming true.

Don't overlook what's happening the computer systems, AI like ChatGPT, banking, commerce, finance everything is interconnected. But God also has a system. Humanity has three kingdoms: the kingdom of God, the kingdom of darkness (Satan's kingdom), and humanity's kingdom. Satan works through humanity. There's something to all this: government and world events. Although it was tough to grasp until things played out, we can say that now.

We must stay focused on the lasting truth amidst the debate and attempt to downplay or dismiss it. The history of belief is that God is in charge. I'll say God is in charge, but He gives us a certain amount of control. Christ will return, and believers should maintain hope and diligence while waiting for His return. Look at the signs we already discussed. There is one more sign we will get into: the weather. There are scriptures for that as well. Be sure to take notes on Daniel 7 and read the entire book.

You'll notice symbolism, but pay close attention to verse 25—there's something you might not have picked up on. Also, check out Daniel 9:25 and Revelation 13. Ask God for clarity on these passages, and others like Revelation 12. Keep in mind that the books of the Bible aren't always presented in chronological order.

There's a lot of prophecy in the Bible. Some have already come true. If you're Spirit-Filled, you might wonder what's happening in the world, the church, and the government. But I believe some of you can admit, just like the Bible says, "I got the Holy Spirit." I didn't just start pretending I really received the Holy Spirit. Some of you are Spirit-filled, too.

So, enjoy it.

Now here we go again. Lastly, we want to discuss the weather and Bible prophecy. I often look at other interpretations and compare them with my own, and I see that sometimes it can be surprising to see someone who shares the same point of view as I do.

See, when it comes to scriptures and the end times, last days, last time, death, etc., all of that has to do with the end times. But there's the common denominator or should I say two the Holy Spirit (Revelation) and the written text. And most of us will agree that we believe Jesus Christ is the world's Savior. He went to Calvary and shed His blood. We believe in the death, burial, and resurrection. So, we believe there will be a finale when we look at all these things. The scriptures compare end-time prophecy to a woman in labor pains(symbolically), but they also talk about the whole creation things many believe will precede Christ's return.

Whether you think in a pre-, mid-, or post-tribulation, scholars will agree with that when it comes to the birth pains because it's written in the scriptures as a comparison.

And we who look at it understand that when a woman is getting ready to deliver the baby, it is one pain after another; the pains get more severe, and they're more consistent. Now, for some of you ladies out there, you can relate to that, and that's how it compares the frequency and the intensity of that. In the Bible, "birth pains" is used metaphorically to describe the suffering and turmoil preceding significant events, particularly the end times. And that's what the Bible does. It tells us that, like the Olivet Discourse of Saint Matthew 24 and 7, Luke 21:11, it predicts increased famines, earthquakes, and widespread sufferings—like plagues. Sometimes, God sends plagues.

Through the scriptures, we can see that God sends plagues throughout the land because of people's disobedience. According to scripture, like the children of Israel, humanity has been punished in times past through earthquakes, famine, and widespread suffering, which can be defined as severe weather events like storms, heat waves, and cosmic disturbances.

And you know, when you really think about it, the Bible mentions unusual signs in the sun, the moon, the stars, and the roaring of the sea and the waves. And I believe some people look the other way and think it's always been this way. But when we think about climate change and seasonal changes, I remember hearing this years ago: seasonal changes will be hotter than ever. A period of significant celestial and atmospheric upheaval the turbulences that people are experiencing on planes, the dryness in the sunrise, and how rivers are drying up.

One minute, we have all this flooding; the next, dryness. The Bible speaks about the Euphrates River drying up. You know, climate change and the earth's distress earthquakes and there's so much happening.

Years ago, some prophets predicted major earthquakes in California because it sits on a fault; honestly, it is Bible prophecy. There have been earthquakes in unusual places like Georgia that are less common. Storms, heavy rains, tornadoes, and hurricanes that devastate entire cities have occurred, including the recent deadly flooding in Texas during the Fourth of July weekend. This affected the Texas Hill Country and surrounding areas.

Kerrville is the largest city in Kerr County, about 100 miles west of Austin. Floodwaters from the Guadalupe River also tragically impacted Camp Mystic, a summer camp for girls in Hunt. People died because of torrential rain, and innocent kids also drowned.

We cannot deny that people are dying. They died in floods, swept away in dormitories, if I can say inside those dormitories where multiple people were packed together. Multiple dormitories, people on vacation homes for the holiday, the 4th of July, around that time. If you study Bible prophecy, many things happened or took place during the Feast of Pentecost, the Feast of Trumpets, and the Feast of Passover according to the Jewish calendar. Consider, everyone.

Some believe that Jesus will return on the Feast of Trumpets, a Jewish feast. Think about it, everyone. But we're not talking about those things. We're discussing the intense weather events as the fulfillment of these prophecies. Even governments around the world have caused a major drought for farmers. The cost of eggs, the cost of this, the cost of that. In some countries, there's a food shortage.

People are dying of starvation. We cannot control the weather. I don't believe we can. Maybe some people think we can, but we cannot. It is a sign of the earth suffering right before our eyes. But I believe God is in charge, though He's given us a certain amount of control. I think that some people will move into a spiritual kingdom mindset. Some will be able to discern the times in which we live.

There's a conference called Because of The Times I feel everyone should research. The failure of reading and teaching on the subject matters dealing with the end of times has caused us not to know the seasons and hour in which we live. See, Jesus lamented; He cried that people could interpret the skies' appearance to predict the weather but failed to interpret the present time and spiritual signs of His coming. And how the weather played a role, or will play a role, in that.

We need to warn the people to manifest repentance to cry out to God. It's not a coincidence that we saw our financial brains in America's World Trade Center come to rubble. I would cite Rabbi Jonathan Cahn, who said it was a harbinger. I think he speaks about seven or nine different harbinger events that would take place before another significant event.

Is it possible that God is warning us with all that we see? Is it possible that our leader, who's connecting with dictators, wants to be a dictator himself? Judge it for yourself.

What are we going to do? Hello? Will we sit idly by and not look at these things slightly closer? I want you to get your Bible and do your own research. Please don't take my word for it. Do your own research. I've given you, I've cited scriptures. Whether you have a King James Version, NLT, or something else NIV don't just use one or two Bible tools. You have a phone. Look up the symbolic meanings of this.

Again, even when you think about Jonah, even when you think about Noah, those were weather events. Judge for yourself. Inevitable storms had specific names. Even when Paul was on that ship, he said, "Abide in the ship." They abided in the boat, and no lives were lost, and they floated on broken pieces.

So, like I said, don't be looking for a rapture. It will happen when it happens.

What? Make up your mind. I've got enough information to prepare and to endure the church, the world, or should I say the church, the government/world events, and the weather.

Now you take the time and judge it for yourself. Are all these things coincidental? That's all.

Chapter 4

Understanding the Signs
Jesus Christ Gave to Mankind

Jesus made many prophecies about the events leading up to and including His second coming. These serve as preludes or signs indicating that His return is near. Jesus spoke about an increase in natural disasters frequent and intensified earthquakes in various places, widespread hunger, starvation, plagues, and diseases that would afflict the last days. We can also interpret a famine for the Word of God as part of these signs. As Scripture says, humanity is destroyed for lack of knowledge because they reject knowledge. Today, people are always learning but never truly coming into the knowledge of the truth.

Many will come claiming to be Christ, deceiving many. When reading this passage in the Gospel of Matthew, it's important to note that Jesus specifically said they would come in His name, not in the names of other religious figures like Buddha or Hare Krishna. This indicates that He spoke primarily to Jewish believers who accepted Him as the Messiah.

This message also applies to us because we believe Jesus is the Messiah. I encourage you to study and highlight this scripture carefully. Many who have done so realize that Jesus is addressing believers who are born again, those following Him closely, even if only a small group. They privately asked Jesus, "When will these things happen? What will be the signs of Your coming and the end of the age?" Reflect on that question. As many have mentioned, natural disasters will increase and become more frequent storm after storm, earthquake after earthquake like childbirth contractions. We are experiencing weather patterns that bring turmoil.

Additionally, diseases such as COVID-19, various viruses, and cancers continue to threaten us, and we still lack cures for common illnesses like colds. Wars and rumors of wars will escalate, along with increasing hatred and iniquity, causing love to grow cold.

Wars and conflicts will intensify, and there will be a rise in deception through false prophets, especially within the church. We are witnessing an unprecedented explosion of individuals claiming to be prophets, apostles, pastors, and bishops many with their own agendas. These are all signs of the end times. People will claim to speak for God but often serve other agendas, such as greed and the love of money, which is the root of all evil. Jesus warned us of these signs, and I urge you to take note.

Are you seeing an explosion of churches and religious leaders claiming authority? Some of what they say may come to pass, but from a different source perhaps deception. As a fruit inspector, I encourage you to observe the signs around you and discern truth from falsehood. Believing what you see and hear is vital because these are clear indicators of our times. Further, Jesus' spoke of signs in the heavens events involving the sun, moon, and stars—that will signal His return.

These signs may occur before, during, or after the tribulation, an intense period of suffering and chaos worldwide, not just in America. Lawlessness will increase dramatically, with crime and murder surging, leading to a society where love grows cold and selfishness dominates. As you observe the suffering around you children starving abroad, economic disparities you can see that this is a global issue, not just an American problem.

Despite America's reputation as a Christian nation, we must ask ourselves: Are we truly a godly nation? What are we doing to uphold biblical principles? The love of many has waxed cold, partly because of how foreigners and less fortunate people are treated. The Bible warns us to be careful how we entertain strangers. America sings of divine grace and brotherhood from sea to sea, but our actions often contradict those ideals, especially toward people in Mexico, Africa, Haiti, and other nations. Judge for yourself.

When believers align themselves with corruption or fail to help the poor, it can invoke God's judgment. The signs of these last days are everywhere. Many will turn away from sound doctrine, preferring to follow teachers who tell them what they want to hear. Hebrews 10:25 warns us not to forsake assembling, but many ignore that and drift into false teachings. Hebrews 6 reminds us that returning to repentance is challenging if we fall away once we have known the truth. Romans 1:21-22 speaks of knowing God but rejecting Him, leading to futile minds.

Additionally, 1 Timothy 4:1 warns that in the last days, some will depart from the faith, giving heed to seducing spirits and doctrines of demons. I urge you, brethren, to present your bodies as sacrifices holy and acceptable to God (Romans 12:1-2). Do not conform to this world's patterns but be transformed by renewing your mind. Many afflictions are common to the righteous, but the Lord promises to deliver us from them all.

Recognize the signs around you spiritually, socially, politically, and environmentally and understand what they mean. Ask yourself: Are we running out of time to get it right? Are we manifesting a form of godliness but denying its power (2 Timothy 3:1-5)? The Bible warns us to turn away from such pretenses. In the last days, men will love themselves and pleasures more than God. This is a perilous time; many are vulnerable to deception even believers.

The twisting of grace, as seen in some teachings, can lead people astray. Titus 2:11 reminds us that the grace of God teaches us to deny ungodliness and worldly lusts. Remember, just as in the days of Noah and Lot, life will continue until the Son of Man returns. Look around at your local churches do they truly follow Jesus? Are believers willing to deny themselves, take up their crosses, and follow Him? Or have we become selfish and self-centered? Could there be the last days?

Lawlessness, including spiritual lawlessness, is rampant. These signs are meant to warn and guide us. They reveal the importance of understanding Jesus' warnings to prepare ourselves spiritually. It's time to get things in order, repent, and call on Jesus surrendering fully to Him before it's too late. The Bible describes the narrow way few will find it compared to the broad road many choose.

As you observe the world, the governments, the weather, and the prophetic signs, ask yourself: What do these signs tell us about Jesus' imminent return? Ignoring these warnings only increases the risk of being deceived. Stay vigilant, study the Scriptures diligently, and prepare your heart. The signs are evident; the time is short.

Make sure you are ready for His coming!

Chapter 5

Are We There Yet?

Many seem to be asking, "Are we there yet?" In this context, "there" refers to the rapture. But what does that mean, and who are they asking? As I mentioned, some believe in a pre-tribulation rapture, others think it will happen mid-tribulation, and others believe in a post-tribulation rapture. We are already in the tribulation period. However, all three views could be interpreted as "Yes, we are there. "Eschatology often involves the end of all things, including death.

Some people believe we are already in that final phase, but a few other events still need to occur. Years ago, I remember hearing people mention that certain events must occur before the rapture. Others insisted that nothing else must happen before the church is taken up. Since many do not believe in a pre-tribulation rapture-the church being taken before the tribulation I often ask: How do you define "church"?

Many churches Baptist, Methodist, Pentecostal, Apostolic, and others—hold various beliefs. Is the "church" a specific denomination, or is it the body of believers, regardless of denomination? I see the church primarily as an institution a place of worship, a community of love and fellowship. But we are ultimately citizens of God's kingdom; the sooner people embrace that reality, the better.

So, are we there yet? Yes. The love of many has grown cold; people are more lovers of themselves than lovers of God. Sin is spreading rapidly not only in the world and our communities but even within churches and places of worship.

Are we there yet? When examining Bible prophecy and what has been written, the answer seems to be "Yes." But then the question becomes, "Where do we go from here? What's next? What still needs to happen?"

Let me say this: you can die at any moment. According to Scripture, after death comes judgment. So, are we there yet? Considering how things are progressing, we are further along than ever in fulfilling what has been prophesied. These messages are not meant to cause anger or anxiety but to warn. This book promises to wake you and your family.

If there's any chance, I might be correct, it's time for you to wake up and realize that, right now, you still have an opportunity to do God's will. I do not set dates or try to predict the exact timing of Christ's return. The Bible clearly states that no one knows the day or the hour. However, the Spirit of Christ in us can quicken our hearts and senses. There is a sense in the air that something is happening, and I can feel it everywhere. Yes, we are there naturally, but are you there spiritually? Do you hear the sirens? Do you hear the alarm calling, "Wake up, Zion"?

The Parable of the Ten Virgins illustrates this: five wise and five foolish. The wise kept their lamps filled and were prepared; the foolish thought they had time. Are we in that place now?

Yes, a great awakening is needed. Are we there yet? Yes. The love of many has grown cold. Are we there yet? Yes. But you must judge for yourself. Observe the signs, experience the times, and measure where you stand. Look around, compare what the Scriptures say, and ask yourself honestly: Are we there yet?

From my perspective, I don't see how we're not there. But I am not God. As you age, you realize you are closer to eternity, just one heartbeat, one breath away. Yes, you are there. You may think, "I don't want to leave this world. I want things to stay the same forever." But the world is changing right before our eyes, and what we have chosen or not chosen to do about it is crucial.

If I were you, I would look around, seek someone who can help explain this question clearly, and pay attention to what's happening in the news, on the radio, in your community, and at your workplace.

Things are about to get rough. Soon, Lord Jesus, that's all I can say. You must be ready and stay ready. Don't get entangled in the cares of this world or the unfruitful works of darkness. Remember what Jesus said: "Depart from me, ye workers of iniquity, for I never knew you"—meaning a genuine relationship.

Yes, I believe we are there. But if you're not yet ready, start getting prepared now. I love you with the love of Jesus. Stay tuned because the trumpet of God may sound at any moment.

Think about it. And if not, endure hardship as a good soldier. Love everybody, keep your head up, and keep a song in your heart.

Yes, I believe we are there.

Chapter 6

The Man of Sin (Lawless One)

Let's now examine the topic of the lawless one in II Thessalonians, chapter two. I believe Paul addresses this subject by suggesting that he's referring to the same person. While some scholars and Bible teachers disagree with my view, I think a system will develop where people worship this evil individual, often called the man of sin or the lawless one. I also believe Satan will possess a man, as the Bible predicts a one-world government, currency, and religion in the end times.

Although the Bible doesn't explicitly use these terms, it proves they will exist during the Antichrist's reign. Think about the apocalyptic vision John describes in Revelation. He sees the beast, which many identify as the Antichrist, embodying power and authority qualities that can't be associated with Christ, who represents love, forgiveness, and compassion. The Antichrist will try to be God despite opposing Christ.

Revelation 13:1 describes him rising from the sea, with seven heads and ten horns. You can also look at Daniel 7:16-24, which describes similar governance systems, representing kings or rulers with authority. When Israel wanted a human king, God was their ruler, but they chose a physical king, leading to Saul. God gave them what they requested, but it didn't turn out well. I don't believe it's solely about one person, but this individual will unite different rulers and dictators, leading to a one-world government. I've discussed this before. This person will wage war against God's people and conquer them (Revelation 13:7).

Over the years in ministry, I've heard of the ten-nation confederacy mentioned in Daniel 2:41-42, representing the ten toes of the statue that makes up the final world system. It may be hard to understand, and I'm not an expert, but many teachings and interpretations attempt to identify the nations involved.

The ten-toed nations will come together in some way, forming a coalition. Revelation 13:7-8 states that the beast will defeat three of them, and the others will serve him. According to prophecy, a coalition will form, and some nations will resist the Antichrist, trying to oppose his spirit. Revelation also contains a lot of symbolism.

Some may disagree with specific interpretations, but if you observe what unfolds, you might recognize it in the characteristics of a conqueror and destroyer who opposes obedience. Does that remind you of anyone? John describes the rulers of this empire as having power and great authority, which they're given. The Bible also talks about the false prophet, who will perform miracles, signs, and wonders, empowered by Satan (Revelation 13:2). This ruler will receive worship from all the world, every tribe, language, and nation (Revelation 13:3-4).

It may seem repetitive, but I encourage you to read and judge for yourself. This person will likely lead a recognized one-world government, sovereign over others. Today, nations are willing to give up some sovereignty to handle crises. Could the United States be the modern-day or even Mystery Babylon? According to the Bible, a global crisis will push nations to embrace anyone promising solutions, and Satan will empower this individual.

He will have control of some people who don't believe in Satan, but you should judge for yourself. This person will gain power because Satan needs a vessel. Remember when Satan entered Judas (Luke 22:3). There will be an establishment of absolute control, and this individual will desire worship and praise. Satan's main goal was to be like God (Isaiah 14:12-14). Controlling money and commerce is part of this plan, so I discuss the one-world currency described in Revelation 13.

This system's religion will be inclusive, accepting all faiths. Revelation 13 explains how everyone, rich and poor, free and enslaved, will be forced to receive a mark on their right hand or forehead, or the name of the beast, to buy or sell (Revelation 13:16). Most people will take the mark out of necessity for food and survival.

This new system will dominate commerce and resources worldwide. It's no coincidence that a man is creating his own cryptocurrency, a universal, mandatory coin tied to the beast's worship (Revelation 13:15). How will this mark be imposed? It could be a chip, a card, or some other technology. Today's tech identifies us at airports and stores, so it's plausible. Revelation also hints at the possibility of the beast's name being associated with the mark. The technology exists now to make all this happen. Many believe the rapture will occur before these events unfold, but others think they'll be left behind.

If the rapture happens, some will be taken, and others will go to face the chaos, an excruciating choice: accept the mark or face persecution and starvation. Many will die for Christ rather than submit. To be a true believer, you must be born again. Some ask if the Holy Spirit will be removed, as suggested in 2 Thessalonians 2. It's unclear, but I believe some faithful will possibly stand against the Antichrist as a testimony of Elijah and Moses.

They will face great persecution for their faith. If these prophecies are accurate, we see the spirit of lawlessness working now and the stage being set. II Thessalonians 2 says God will send strong delusion to those who refuse the truth. Could you be one of the deceived? Judge for yourself. People are already under a spell, but I believe that spell can be broken through Jesus' power.

I pray it is today, as you read this. In Jesus' name, Amen.

Chapter 7

Israel's Role in Bible Prophecy

We might as well discuss Israel's role according to Bible prophecy. In the Bible, Israel plays a vital role as the nation through which God's covenant promises and plan of redemption are fulfilled, especially regarding the Messiah and a future kingdom on earth. Bible prophecy refers to Israel's national rebirth and the eventual establishment of a kingdom in Israel. When we read about Israel, we see they are recognized as God's chosen people.

That is a fact according to our Christian Bible, where God made a promise to Abraham because Abraham proved his faithfulness to God. So, God favored Abraham, widely regarded as the "father of faith." Three groups of people descended from Abraham, Ishmael, and Isaac. Even though Ishmael was born of the bondwoman, God stated in your Bible that He would bless them. And, of course, you know how God will bless Isaac, the promised child from whom these nations and peoples will come.

There is another group of people who come from Abraham, not only the Jews but also those who become Abraham's children by faith, trusting in God. This is the promise God gave Abraham, where you find the prophecy about the Messiah. John 1 says, "In the beginning was the Word, and the Word was God." It then describes how the Word became flesh and dwelt among us. It further says that many who received Him were given power to become the sons of God. So, we are grafted into the prophecy of the Messiah's coming. The Scripture states that there is neither Jew nor Greek.

Therefore, we should be thankful to God for our position. Israel also plays a crucial role in the end times, including events of persecution and the protection God has provided for Israel over the years, such as during the Six-Day War.

God preserved this small group of people and will be a significant part of the global Gospel mission. People worldwide visit Israel to see Golgotha, the Upper Room, and many historic sites where Paul, Peter, and the other disciples were, including their tombs. Even the media is paying attention to rebuilding the temple, which was prophesied, and the sacrifices that will be offered. It has been reported that they have already found a red heifer to conduct the sacrifices.

Many biblical and prophetic events are unfolding that we can read about and learn from, yet many of us are not being taught these things. God told Israel, "You are my covenant people." He made a promise and established them as His chosen people to fulfill His covenant promises and to deliver His Word and the Messiah to the world. Remember that in 1948, God said, "I'm going to return my people, Israel, back to their homeland," because Israel became scattered due to their disobedience.

But God made a promise: He would bring them back and restore them. It would be a rebirth. Due to their disobedience, God told Abraham that his seed would be strangers in a land that was not theirs, serving for about 400 years, after which they would come out with great substance. This is Bible prophecy. I want y'all to think about this. Study the history of Israel.

You can look at the Bible's account of Israel, but also examine the historical events, like in 1948, when the League of Nations approved the nation of Israel, even though Israel didn't have land before that. This was the fulfillment of prophecy concerning Israel's rebirth as a nation. This also relates to the hostility some nations have toward Israel. Even now, many Muslim countries refuse to recognize Israel.

They want to erase Israel from the map, and if they could, it would have already happened. Consider Iran, Persia, Iraq, ancient Babylon, and I would even include Russia.

That's why we see the conflict unfolding right before our eyes in Gaza. Does that mean the people in power will do the right thing? God has removed kings before, and I believe He will do so again. Meanwhile, God's plan is unfolding, just like in the old days.

You read in Revelation about the big dragon and other symbols, but I don't want to get ahead of myself. Despite all this, God has looked out for His people. Notice that Jesus came to the Jews first. He came to them first, but they rejected Him. So, Jesus turned and embraced whoever would come. "He came to His own, but His own received Him not." The Gospel was opened to the Gentiles through their rejection, forming the Church. Some call the Church "spiritual Israel," while others don't believe in that term.

Jesus said He would send another Helper, the Holy Spirit, who will abide with believers forever if the Spirit leads them.

We see the transition from the Jews who rejected Him to the formation of citizens of the kingdom through the death, burial, and resurrection of Jesus Christ, not through the blood of animal sacrifice.

Some Orthodox Jews still do not accept Jesus as the Messiah. I'll give you a little history. We see the formation of the ecclesia, the called-out ones. While the Church consists of believers from all nations, some see it as spiritual Israel, separate from ethnic Israel. However, I believe that, according to the Bible, Israel still holds a unique place in God's prophetic plan. Israel plays a key role in Bible prophecy, even in the final battle, the valley of Megiddo, when Jesus returns and defeats a group of wicked people. You can read about this in Ezekiel 37, where Israel became a nation, and God says He will bring them back (Ezekiel 38).

God even says He will put a hook in the jaw of those who come against His people to destroy them all. I recommend that some people read chapters 37 and 38 of Ezekiel. Additionally, Ezekiel 33 discusses a guard, and I believe there are guards today. You must understand that Israel holds a significant role and position in Bible prophecy. Some people want to destroy Israel and try to divide the land.

This is part of the end times and the fulfillment of prophecy. Those who study will see that this is called "comparative study." As Austin said, we call this the time of the Church, the church age, but many scholars and theologians believe the door of the Church will eventually close, and God will return to His chosen people. We can see the pieces of the puzzle coming together. The Psalms say the temple has already started being built, but they can't even pray on the Temple Mount without big attacks.

You see news about conflicts in Gaza, much of which relates to Bible prophecy. Chapter 9 of the Book of Daniel discusses the Antichrist and how he will enter the temple, acting as if he were God.

It's not a coincidence that most Jews don't believe Jesus is the Messiah. It's also striking how close our president is to Putin and the prime minister of Israel at the same time. That's why, when I look at the Abraham Accords, which brokered a peace treaty, I notice that the dollar was part of that treaty.

According to scholars and Bible prophecies not biased men and women the Antichrist will break that treaty and turn completely against Israel. I wonder who that might be. Judge for yourself. Then there's the Church. Some in the Church believe in replacement theology, also known as Super Sensationalism. It's a Christian belief that the Church has replaced ethnic Israel as God's chosen people through the new covenant, fulfilling and nullifying the old covenant.

Many believe that Israel's unique spiritual status is no longer valid. While this view is widely held in Christian history, it has faced significant criticism and reevaluation in recent generations. In other words, many Christians believe that God no longer needs Israel because they rejected Him. He replaced Israel with the Church. I see this as anti-Semitic and a distortion of biblical texts about Israel, their role, and promises. You can look up replacement theology yourself.

It teaches that the Church, through faith in Jesus Christ, has replaced Israel as God's chosen people. What do y'all think about that? We receive His blessings and promises as the Church, but we are divided and scattered when you look at the Christian Church. How can that be when the Church is so divided even in its relationship with Jesus Christ? So, some of you should do your research on replacement theology. You might be shocked to learn about it; I know.

Some of you have never heard that term. But it's a movement and a teaching. Could it be that God has said, "Hey, I'm replacing you, Israel, with the Church the believers because you rejected Me"? If that's the case, then you have "mystery Babylon." Could the believers be "mystery Israel," and the Bible no longer refer to Israel literally but as a spiritual institution? Judge for yourself. That would make for an interesting debate and conversation.

Some people believe that all the covenants and promises to Israel are null and void, which makes the latter the only dispensation for Israel's future. It dismisses any importance of the ethnic Jewish people, implying that the unique relationship ended with the rejection of Jesus Christ. The phrase "Super Sensationalism" is often used. There are different forms of it, including punitive ones that claim God is punishing Israel for rejecting Christ.

Now I'm getting into theology, but many believe Old Testament texts have limited relevance for forming Christian convictions today. Arguments against replacement theology say it misreads critical biblical passages, especially Romans 11, which they believe confirms God's unchangeable gift and calling for Israel and His everlasting promises to them.

Many Christians believe that God's promises to the Jewish people, including the land of Israel, are eternal and that the Church has not replaced Israel in God's plan. Historically, this doctrine has fueled anti-Jewish hatred and distorted the Bible's message. It emphasizes inclusion, not replacement. An alternative view argues that, rather than replacing Israel, the Church includes all believers Jewish and Gentile who are heirs to the promises made to Abraham through faith.

Thus, this specific theological belief or doctrine has many different interpretations. But many of us believe that Israel has a role to play in these last days, especially concerning the battle of Armageddon and the return of Jesus Christ. Is it possible? Jesus stated in the New Testament that you must come through Him to be saved. This can be challenging for the average believer. So, here is a lesson on replacement theology and Israel's role in Bible prophecy.

Those born-again believers, including Messianic Jews, believe Jesus is the Messiah. The disciples were all Jews. According to your Bible, when Jesus spoke with them on the Mount (the Sermon on the Mount), they recognized Jesus as the Messiah. I hope everyone seeks Him, surrenders to Him, and does their best in these last days because there is also an apostate church. Apostasy means a church that deceives people a group that believes in another Jesus.

Read 2 Corinthians 11:2, which talks about "another gospel," "another Jesus," and "another spirit" being preached. You can judge that for yourself. I believe we are heading home, people. The signs are all around us, and I genuinely believe it. What you're reading will change how you think and understand Bible prophecy isn't about fortune-telling or material things, but about the Spirit of God and spiritual people who serve God during this time. Here's the truth: Israel still has a role in this hour, and so do you born-again believers.

Chapter 8

Is America and Donald Trump

Fulfilling Bible Prophecy?

Many questions have been asked by people, some of which reveal confusion about Bible prophecy. Bible prophecy is essential to our Christian faith and supports our beliefs, although many are sometimes not exposed to it. It's a fact that Christianity often depends on faith and experience. Many events written in the Scriptures have already happened, whether you believe it or not. Prophecy encompasses the past, present, and future.

Some things in the Bible have already occurred. Others are happening now right as I speak. And still, some are yet to come. One common question is whether America is mentioned in the Scriptures. We often say Great Britain is in the Scriptures. But do you realize that America came out of Great Britain, out of Europe? America is 249 years old. At the end of the day, we can see the role our country plays at this moment. I often say that America is one of the most Christian nations in the world. Judge that for yourself one of the most Christian nations in the world.

And we'll celebrate 250 years of being a country next year. You know, God has truly shared His grace with us. I mentioned that in another chapter, but I would be grateful if you could read it repeatedly. How can America not somehow be mentioned in the Bible? Not by name, but through its characteristics. It's what you call a providential nation. A providential nation or country is one that displays certain traits, even if its name isn't in the Bible. Many things are not recorded in the Bible, like the airplane, train, automobile, drive-in movie, TV, radio, and telephone.

Those aren't named in your Bible either. Many cities aren't mentioned in the Bible as well. But could it be possible that its characteristics are there even though America isn't mentioned by name? Some feel that identifying America as Mystery Babylon is just based on interpretation. Some Christians believe this conclusion is drawn from the characteristics and interpretation of eschatology.

If you read the context of Revelation chapters 17 and 18, it describes a great Mystery Babylon. Some people believe this is not ancient Babylon, because there was a known ancient Babylon of which we know but Mystery Babylon remains a mystery. It is Symbolic. While the ancient city of Babylon is a real place, Mystery Babylon is generally seen as a symbolic nation. If you study or research Mystery Babylon, you'll find a lot of information. It discusses how powerful and corrupt it is. It describes a worldly system that can serve as a metaphor for a specific nation or, as some say, an empire.

Even though we don't call America an empire or use the term empire, we don't often think about the system in place the financial system and the diversity of religions. We don't have a king yet. I think Donald wants to be a king, but we are a capitalist society and a capitalist country. Our currency is not backed by gold or anything else. Once it was, but now it's a fiat currency.

Fiat means it's not supported by anything, and they can print as much as they want. That's why, during COVID, they issued stimulus checks. Stimulus checks were intended to boost the country's economy because you pay taxes and buy goods, among other reasons. That's why our country has free commerce and free trade. It seems like this is coming to a quick end, at least to some extent, because I believe we are heading toward or are already in a cancel culture society. I think America is leading the way because it's a superpower.

As I mentioned in my previous writings, I can see the collaboration. Think about Putin, Trump, and Benny from Israel. They're trying to remove the prime minister. The other day, it occurred to me that these three men and others are part of a corrupt system that favors the wealthy. This relates to America, the banking system, and various established systems Social Security, Medicare, and Medicaid.

America has naturally prospered for some, but not everyone. Now, this is a topic of debate, depending on interpretation. Some scholars see America, or Babylon, as a symbol for Rome or the Roman Empire, or simply as a universal emblem of worldly power and corruption. When you consider Mystery Babylon based on context and interpretation, the idea stems from the book of Revelation, which uses much symbolic language. Not everything in the book is literal.

Mystery Babylon represents a powerful country, nation, or group of idolatrous and spiritually corrupt people. It is a system that persecutes the righteous and is ultimately destroyed by God. Some individuals, churches, pastors, and bishops see the United States as fulfilling Mystery Babylon in Bible prophecy because of its perceived global power, moral corruption, and influence over other countries.

Suppose you examine comparisons in Daniel 9 and Revelation 17 and 18. In that case, they appear to warn Christians of our dangers and risks our perilous position and the danger of aligning our loyalty with worldly institutions instead of God's kingdom. Let's be honest: we have moved away from the foundation of righteousness. As I often say, we are a Christian country, but are we a godly country? Some interpret the Roman Empire symbolically, including its landmass and ports that connect different regions.

When we look at America, we see some powerful ports where ships come and go on nearly every side of the country. Ports like Galveston, Houston, near water, New York City, South Carolina, Fort Lauderdale, and Miami stand out. Consider this could America be Mystery Babylon? Then look at the corruption, politics, economy, and systems. Throughout history, America has been a Pacific nation.

But how can America be overlooked without having a place in history? I want y'all to judge for yourselves. I often say, "Comparative study, comparative study." Now, what are we going to do? Are we just going to ignore the possibility and probability? I'm not talking about absolute certainty.

When we observe our leaders, some exhibit the traits of a wannabe king someone who is not truly Christlike. Based on his rhetoric, he tears things apart, makes changes, and aligns with countries whose presidents and leaders are dictators.

So, is America in Bible prophecy not by name, but perhaps by its characteristics? Does the name mention its leader? No. But look at his character. Make the application to America and its ports, and see if anything matches America. Is America and Donald Trump fulfilling a part of Bible prophecy?

According to Daniel 9, Revelation 13, 17, and 18, that is a fascinating question. I guess y'all know that Satan will embody someone. But I thank y'all.

Chapter 9

One World Government,

Currency and Religion

All right, my friends, this chapter discusses a one-world government, one-world currency, and I like to say one-world religion one, one, one. Now, the Bible talks about the future, and as we discussed earlier, it mentions the collaboration of various governments, uniting all the superpowers under one, including economic control.

In the book of Daniel, which is a prophetic book just like Revelation, though it doesn't use those exact terms, we can see Daniel describing a future powerful empire an empire represented by beasts with 10 horns. At the same time, Revelation describes the beast, the Antichrist, who is given authority over every nation and enforces the mark required for buying and selling. Therefore, this relates to a system that will be in place for people to buy and sell. Daniel's chapter 7, verses 23 to 25, describes a one-world government.

When we think about the superpowers Putin, Biden, and the current President of the United States, Donald Trump we see some of the most powerful nations. We could also include North Korea and China, some of the world's most influential countries. When we consider the dictators in today's world, it seems like only one nation doesn't have a dictatorship because we've traditionally been known as a democracy.

However, we are quickly moving toward a time when democracy might fade. We have a leader in office who seems to want to be a king and a dictator. Just look at his actions. And the Bible talks about these kinds of things. Now, what we're discussing is focused. Daniel 7:23-25 describes the fourth beast, which is very different from the others. Now, with 10 horns there's an 11th, powerful horn and it can devour the whole earth, tread it down, and break it into pieces.

Many scholars and theologians interpret this as a future world power under the control of the Antichrist. Revelation 13:2 and 8. Remember, this relates to John the Revelator on the island of Patmos. John sees the beast that receives authority from the dragon, which is considered Satan.

I know that debates can arise about the symbolic meanings in Scriptures. But I hoped you could bear with me for a few minutes while I read. I always stress this and will repeat it: comparative study.

The dragon, representing Satan, rules over every tribe, people, language, and nation. In other words, this ruler and authoritarian figure receive worldwide worship and exercises global dominance. This is tied to the concept of a one-world religion. So, you have a one-world government, one-world currency, and one-world religion. It is fair to say this is described in Revelation 13:16-17.

The Bible doesn't use these terms, but let's examine them more closely. A one-world currency can be linked to a system of economic control where a mark of the beast is a mark that causes you to have an idea attached or something that will identify you to buy or sell. In other words, nobody can participate in commerce without this mark, which will be universal and mandatory, affecting all humanity regardless of their financial status or social connections.

Now, interpretation and context can be critical. Sometimes, these scriptures are misunderstood as descriptions of future events, specifically a tribulation period during which there will be and we are already at that point a global system established by the Antichrist, enforced by those involved in a dictatorship. That's why it's crucial for people and we're emphasizing this today to place their people in key positions.

When we examine the Tower of Babel in Genesis 11, some may see this as a foreshadowing of a unified effort against God's authority. If you read that, they say, "We're going to build a tower that reaches all the way up to heaven," a building. In other words, some scholars and theologians suggest they contemplated building something so high that they would not be affected if a flood came as God's judgment. This was meant to prevent or serve as a safeguard, so they could say, "God, you won't get us again," challenging God's authority. But God dwarfed their plans. Because, as it says in the book, He said, "Let us go down and see what these folks are doing."

Summarizing, when God saw what humanity was up to, He said, "If we don't confuse their language. There's nothing they won't be able to do." What a statement. That may be hard for some to understand because we often say God is in charge. But I say God is in charge, and He gives us a certain amount of control.

However, He has given humanity the ability of free will, that is, to control and do things according to their will instead of the will of God. For example, Jesus in the garden is a high example. He says, "Lord, not my will, but Thy will be done. Not my will, but Thy will be done." Now, judge that for yourself.

God said there was nothing they wouldn't be able to do. This suggests that God has allowed humanity to act outside His will. That's how the one-world government, world currency, and one-world religion came into being. Now, God confused their tongues. God established human projects that are not aligned with divine will. It's clear that you have a will judge it for yourself. So, you have a one-world government. Coalitions and collaborations with superpowers are forming right now. Regarding currency, cryptocurrency has surged dramatically.

Now, is it possible that we're approaching the point where these men these four kings or kingdoms these super, superpowers, which we read about not in those exact words, but as coming together to create a system? And my friends and brothers, a system is already in place to fulfill this. Judge it for yourself. Think about it very carefully.

Oh, boy, the one-world religion causes all humanity to worship the beast. The universal religion will be about inclusion. That means there isn't just one way, but many ways to what some will call God. And we can see that coming up soon. You know, one world government, one world currency, one world religion. Stop and think for a second. Could we see the connections and won't admit it? This is why you need men and women of God like the sons of Issachar who can discern the times we live in.

We have a banking system and Social Security, and most systems are in place and can be monitored. Credit cards, gold fly on planes, cashless payment options, and even some hotels now operate cashless. So, are we living in a cashless society? Because guess what? You can't monitor cash, but you can scan a credit card. You can't monitor cryptocurrency or digital currency. And this is happening today.

Let's stop ignoring the truth, facts, and these systems already in place, so we can see Daniel 7, 9, and Revelation 13 possibly being fulfilled right before our eyes. Think about it: one world government, one world currency, and one world religion. Please stop trying to dismiss the obvious, and let's see what's about to happen next.

Chapter 10

Satan's Final Attack

Well, my friends, brothers, and sisters, I want to share one of the most powerful books in the Bible: Ezekiel, chapter 37. This chapter is about a vision concerning the valley of dry bones. Many scholars and theologians interpret this book as focusing on Israel's restoration from exile. I know some people associate the part about the dry bones with a broader story that may not be directly related to the text because it specifically addresses the restoration of Israel from exile, where God or His power brings them back to life and reunites the divided kingdoms of Israel and Judah.

These are two Kingdoms God's Kingdoms! the domains of Israel and Judah under King David. The chapter describes the vision of dry bones miraculously coming together to form a living army, symbolizing God's power to restore what appears to be a lifeless nation.

Similarly, Ezekiel shares a second vision in which he takes two sticks, one representing Judah and the other Israel, and joins them together signifying one nation of God but two kingdoms foreshadowing the future unity of the people under God's one King, David. Consider this. When we examine Ezekiel chapters 1 through 14, I will briefly summarize the valley of dry bones.

In a vision, Ezekiel sees a valley full of dry bones, and the text states that these bones symbolize the house of Israel, which is in a state of spiritual and physical death and despair among all those who have been taken into exile. Now, God gives Ezekiel a prophetic message to the bones. What a powerful image! God instructs Ezekiel to prophesy to the bones. Then what happens? The bones come together, and the scripture says they form flesh yet they still have no life. They come together.

Remember, this is a prophetic vision. Sometimes you experience prophetic visions, dreams, and utterances. The vision comes before the utterance. God will give you a vision or a dream, and then He wants you to speak it. Remember, we should always prophesy the prophecy not just randomly about clothes, houses, cars, etc., but learn to prophesy the prophecy by hearing from God.

Then see what happens: the bones come together and are covered with flesh but have no life. Then God commands Ezekiel to prophesy to the breath yes, to the breath, to oxygen, to the wind from the four corners and have it entered the bodies, making them stand up as a living army. In other words, God apparently breathed into them through the wind the breath of life and now they become a mighty army. Remember, this is a vision. The main point is that God will bring His people back to life, physically restoring them to their land and giving them His Spirit to revive them naturally and spiritually.

Now, you can go to your Bible and read Ezekiel 37:15-28. God is still giving Ezekiel instructions to take two wooden sticks. While following God's order, God tells him to write on them: one for Judah and one for Joseph, or Israel. I repeated it I said before, I say it again representing the two kingdoms. He is to hold them together in his hands as if they were one. Look at the vision.

Then God declares that these two sticks will become one in His hand. All of this relates to Bible prophecy. This prophecy and vision describe the future reunification of the United Kingdom into one single nation under King David, who will be the eternal king. Overall, this relates to hope and restoration. This chapter delivers a powerful message of hope to a despairing people, reassuring them that God has not forsaken or abandoned them, but will bring about their physical, national, and spiritual renewal.

If we're honest with ourselves, some of us can see the collaboration God has brought together during this exciting time. God did this. Read it in Ezekiel chapter 37, but also look at chapter 38, which I want you to see as Satan's final attack. We observe the formation of Israel Judah and Israel uniting a prophecy. They are no longer alive, but because Ezekiel speaks prophetically, this is what prophecy does. Prophecy isn't about cars, houses, money, or clothes.

Most people read this specific text without understanding its significance and facts. It talks about the Israeli household coming back together in 1948. Judge it for yourself. This prophetic utterance was written long before 1948, which is why most Bible scholars and theologians accept it. When they see the pieces coming together, they say, "Wow, the Bible is fulfilling itself," just like the sun, the stars, climate change, weather patterns, and seasonal shifts all these are part of Bible prophecy.

Now, let me get through this: Satan's final attack. Ezekiel chapter 38 addresses the prophecy against Gog, an influential leader who will be part of Magog. Some believe Gog is an individual, while others think Gog is a country that will lead a great army from the north. Many also say the north of Israel is Russia. Judge for yourself. Gog will lead a mighty army from the north to attack a restored Israel living in safety. The chapter describes God's active intervention to destroy Gog and his allies with supernatural forces, such as a great earthquake and a rain of fire and hail.

This will set a precedent that causes God to reveal His greatness and holiness to the nations. That chapter contains a prophecy against Gog, and it begins with God's direct message to the prophet Ezekiel to prophesy against Gog, the chief prince of Rosh, Meshech, and Tubal a coalition of nations.

Like I said before, many scholars view this as Russia, with Meshech and Tubal possibly referring to Moscow and other regions. I won't get into all these names you can Google and research them yourself. But it's a coalition of nations. Gog will lead a large army of many countries, including Persia. Persia used to be ancient Iran present-day Iran not Iraq, as some think Ethiopia, Libya, Gomer, and the house of Togarmah from the far north, all attacking the land of Israel. This coalition will come against Israel, which will be in a state of safety during this attack.

This will happen after the Jewish people have been gathered from the nations and will be living safely in the mountains of Israel, which had long been desolate. Before the attack, some of you had already fulfilled this prophecy. We have seen the Jews return to their homeland. Now, what God will do is intervene and defeat Gog and his army, saying that He will turn Gog around, put a hook in his jaw or mouth, and lead him out.

In other words, God will put a hook in their mouth, so they have no choice but to fall prey to God's people. Satan, naturally, according to the scripture, is going to attack God's people. Spiritually, he is attacking them right now in the last days, perilous times shall come. He is attacking their minds and spirits. I believe he has cast spells over people who do not even realize it.

But meanwhile, God will put a hook in Israel's enemies' mouths. A great earthquake will shake the land of Israel, and God will send torrents of rain, hailstones, and burning sulfur on Gog, the troops, and the nations that align themselves with him. This is the sanctification of God's name the setting apart of His reputation and His defense of Israel. God's intervention aims to show His greatness and holiness and reveal Himself to many nations so they will know He is the Lord. That is the final conflict. But there will also be a final attack in the valley of Magog.

There is also an attack on the spiritual man and woman of God, and God will smite the enemy in their part. We are already experiencing a tribulation period possibly the lead-up to tribulation. Now think about this: it's not just Israel, but it's against everyone who calls on the name of the Lord. Remember, Israel rejected God, and according to some Bible scholars and theologians, God will turn back to the nation of Israel.

We see that in Ezekiel chapter 37, Israel becomes a nation. In chapter 38, we see the armies of this world coalition trying to destroy Israel, but God will intervene. For some of you who don't believe in the Rapture, I understand. Some of you have never explored Bible scholar eschatology. I've provided enough information for you to judge for yourself. That's the final conflict both physically and spiritually. Israel has already been restored, and that's a fact. The League of Nations recognized it in 1948, officially making it a nation.

This should excite you, God will always have a people, and we are meant to be that people. There's much more I could say and add, but I won't do that now. I hope you'll tell someone about this book. It needs to be shared everywhere, and I pray you'll give me some feedback. Are these the last days? I believe they are. Has Trump played a role in the past few days? I think he has—more than we'll ever know. Thank you for your time, and I have one question: What if the United States of America is Mystery Babylon?

Judge for yourself!

Conclusion

Everything happening in our world today is very significant. It is crucial to warn people about the possibilities we face, not only from the perspective of the United States but also considering the entire world. Across various nations, we see signs of starvation, violence, murder, earthquakes, storms many of which are beyond our control. Climate change continues to accelerate, and attitudes among men and women are shifting; the love of many is waxing cold and worsening.

Even the church has essentially become a place of entertainment. Most people go about their daily routines, ignoring the obvious, while others view these events more intensely. The battle between good and evil, life and death, remains very real. Many urgent issues are unfolding for which we do not have clear answers. We do not know how these things might culminate soon on this planet; ultimately, all of it relates to people.

We once thought COVID-19 was devastating, but there are other viruses and global events that our world governments may not fully reveal. Some of these incidents cause mass chaos, and we must consider that there are events beyond our understanding. Looking back at what has already occurred, we are approaching some form of conclusion. Artificial intelligence (AI) is advancing so rapidly that it could surpass human intelligence, potentially leading to a robot uprising or a takeover of the world.

Biotechnology is also progressing. Deliberate genetic engineering, the creation of bacteria, and other experiments could result in catastrophic bioweapons or uncontrollable super creatures.

Consider the labs doing this research—some speculate that COVID-19 was created in a laboratory, and others warn that chemical weapons might be in development somewhere. The possibilities are alarming.

Think about recent phenomena like the heat death of the universe, which some scientists predict could occur billions of years from now, when the universe reaches a uniform temperature with no energy remaining. We observe natural disasters earthquakes along fault lines and changing weather patterns—and sense that something significant is happening in the universe. These shifts could spread quickly, like how COVID-19 spread. It seems that some laws of physics are being challenged, threatening to destroy everything we know.

Humanity's knowledge is limited, but there's an undeniable feeling in the air something we can sense but cannot fully understand.

Scientists have proposed scenarios like the "Big Rip," where the universe's expansion accelerates so much that galaxies, stars, and even atoms are torn apart.

Research into theories like the Big Bang and other cosmological models shows that humans are exploring the very fabric of creation and some are even trying to understand or replicate divine creation.

For example, experiments involving genetic manipulation or attempts to create life such as artificial wombs raise profound questions. Some biblical prophecy suggests that humans invent things beyond natural limits, driven by free will. The conclusion about the world's end is not a single event but a complex mix of scientific and religious ideas. Many people get stuck in their specific ideology or theory.

When we look at religion, it's not just Christianity; other faiths also have their own views. For example, some believe that the sun or a cosmic event, like the asteroid Wormwood mentioned in Revelation, could cause the Earth's destruction.

Scientists monitor asteroids like Apophis, which some predicted might hit Earth in 2032, though those predictions have changed. The risk of a final judgment or a major disaster still exists, and different cultures and religions interpret it differently. Hinduism, for example, describes cosmic cycles of creation, preservation, and dissolution, suggesting that the universe undergoes endless rebirths.

Judaism refers to the "end of days" not as final destruction but as a transformation leading to unprecedented peace, sometimes linked to the millennial reign in Christianity. Many believe no one can definitively predict how or when the world will end; instead, we are left with questions and signs.

From a scientific standpoint, predictions about celestial events vary widely. Some say the universe could end billions of years from now, while others believe it could happen sooner, as suggested in the Book of

Revelation. Terms like "blood moon" are connected to prophetic interpretations, implying that cosmic events may signal significant occurrences.

Some theorize that the sun could turn red, vaporize Earth, or trigger catastrophic changes such as massive earthquakes and tsunamis. The biblical reference to Wormwood and the destructive power of nuclear war also reflects current fears. Religious beliefs about the end times vary: Christians expect a final judgment, a new heaven and new earth, with the faithful experiencing eternal life and others facing eternal separation from God. Islam teaches of a resurrection and judgment based on deeds, not just faith in Jesus Christ.

Hinduism views the universe as cycling through creation and destruction, with reincarnation as a central concept. Judaism envisions a future era of peace and restoration after a period of upheaval.

Ultimately, there are no definitive Answers—only questions. Theories abound, ranging from physical destruction to societal collapse, from spiritual upheaval to cosmic renewal.

Some believe that humanity's understanding is limited and that a divine plan or cosmic event may be imminent. I have examined various beliefs in this book, exploring biblical prophecy and secular theories to shape my view. As believers, we are called to prophesy according to the revelations in the Book of Revelation, which warns of consequences for adding to or taking away from Scripture. I share this information not to force beliefs but to encourage personal study and discernment. Looking at current world leaders such as Putin, the President of Russia, North Korea's Kim Jong-un, the Prime Minister of Israel, and others through both natural and spiritual lenses, I am led to consider whether we are approaching a climactic point described in biblical prophecy.

The signs of wars, rumors of war, earthquakes, moral decay, and the love of many growing colds all seem interconnected. The rise of a cashless society, digital currency, and surveillance systems align with prophetic visions of a system that monitors and controls all transactions possibly connected to the Antichrist and global governance.

I urge you to study the Bible and observe our times. Don't just take my word for it; seek understanding for yourself. Some believe that when the Bible speaks about "the last Trump," it could be about an individual symbolizing a leader who initiates the final events. But I am not saying that, but it is food for thought. Is the domino effect already starting? I hope this book offers both natural and spiritual insights. It's not only about America but also about the world we inhabit. As a providential nation, America is crucial; its characteristics and leadership could influence global events.

Whether you call Him Allah, Jesus, or Yeshua, or refer to Him as the divine energy source, the ultimate truth is that all paths lead toward divine judgment.

Some believe that one person or a series of events might end the world as we know it.

Judge for yourself!

"   For I testify unto every man that heareth the words of the prophecy of this book, if any man shall add unto these things, God shall add unto him the plagues that are written in this book: And if any man shall take away from the words of the book of this prophecy, God shall take away his part out of the book of life, and out of the holy city, and *from* the things which are written in this book" Revelation 22:18-19.

Soon Come, Lord Jesus Christ!

REFERENCES

Bible Scholar

- Focus: The scholarly examination and interpretation of the Bible as a text.

- Approach: Employs methods like historical-critical analysis, looking at the Bible's historical, cultural, and literary contexts to understand its original meaning.

- Methodology: May study biblical languages (Hebrew, Greek) and analyze the text's composition, authorship, and internal consistency.

- Assumption: Does not always begin with a faith-based premise, but follows evidence wherever it leads, viewing the Bible as a cultural artifact or historical document.

Christian Scholar

- Focus: Broader academic study informed by Christian faith and tradition.

- Approach: Integrates biblical studies with other aspects of Christian understanding, such as theology, history, and ethics.

- Methodology: Can include biblical studies but also engages with broader theological frameworks and applies Christian virtues, aiming for a holistic understanding of faith.

- Assumption: Grounded in a Christian worldview, with scholarship expected to align with and serve one's faith and the broader Christian community.

Key Differences & Overlap

- Scope: Bible scholarship is a specific academic field, while Christian scholarship is a broader category of academic work within a faith tradition.

- Faith Premise: A Christian scholar operates from a faith perspective, whereas a Bible scholar may or may not.

- Overlap: A Christian scholar often engages in biblical studies as part of their work, and many Bible scholars are also Christians.

- Purpose: A Christian scholar aims to integrate faith and academic inquiry, while a Bible scholar's primary focus is the critical analysis of the text itself.

In Revelation 13:7, the beast from the sea represents a tyrannical governmental power, possibly a future Antichrist, empowered by Satan to persecute and demand worship from God's people. It is a composite of ancient tyrannical empires, depicted as a fearsome, ten-horned, seven-headed creature that claims blasphemous authority and wages war against believers until its inevitable destruction.

Symbolic Representation

- A combination of ancient empires: The beast's features are drawn from the beasts described in Daniel 7, symbolizing robust, oppressive governmental systems that have historically persecuted God's people.

- The Antichrist: Many interpret this beast as a figure known as the Antichrist, a future individual or entity that will embody the ultimate in evil leadership and demand ultimate allegiance.

Key Characteristics and Actions

- Satanic Empowerment: The dragon (Satan) grants the beast its power, throne, and great authority, establishing its rule as a direct opposition to God's power.

- Blasphemous Authority: The beast utters proud words and blasphemies against God and His followers.

- Persecution of Saints: It is given power to make war on God's holy people and to conquer them, with authority over every nation and language.

- Worship: People whose names are not written in the Lamb's Book of Life will worship the beast and the dragon.

Historical and Future Context

- Original Audience: To the first-century audience, the beast was a tangible threat, referring to the tyrannical Roman Empire and its demand for emperor worship.

- Contemporary Relevance: For believers today, the beast represents any hostile government or power that demands ultimate allegiance, requiring obedience to human laws over God's commands.

- Future Fulfillment: Many see the beast also as a prophecy about a future, final form of tyrannical power that will be revealed in the end times.

In Daniel chapter 7, the vision describes four fantastic beasts rising from the sea, each symbolizing a succession of world empires: a lion (Babylon), a bear (Medo-Persia), a leopard (Greece), and a terrible, powerful fourth beast (Rome).

The vision culminates with God establishing His eternal kingdom. The four beasts represent earthly powers that rise and fall under divine design before the saints receive God's everlasting kingdom.

The Four Beasts Explained

- The Lion: Like a lion with eagle's wings, this beast represents the Babylonian Empire, known for its power and conquest. The plucking of the wings symbolizes a loss of strength and dominion.

- The Bear: This lopsided creature, with three ribs in its mouth, symbolizes the Medo-Persian Empire. The bear's brute strength signifies the empire's force, and the ribs represent nations devoured by the Medes and Persians, such as Babylon, Lydia, and Egypt.

- The Leopard: This four-winged, four-headed leopard symbolizes the Greek Empire, spearheaded by Alexander the Great. Its speed reflects the swiftness of Alexander's conquests, and its four heads represent the subsequent division of his empire among his four generals.

- The Fourth Beast: A terrifying, powerful, and unique beast with iron teeth, this creature symbolizes the Roman Empire. It is distinct from the others, representing an empire that crushes and devours, annihilating its enemies.

Significance of the Vision

- Divine Sovereignty: The dream reveals that God is in control, with all human kingdoms rising and falling by His holy will.

- Oppression and Judgment: The beasts represent arrogant and oppressive kings who oppose God.

- The vision shows that these earthly powers will be removed, and God's kingdom will be established.

- The Eternal Kingdom: At the conclusion of the vision, the "Ancient of Days" (God) establishes His eternal kingdom, and the saints will receive this kingdom that will never end.

The Book of Revelation describes the Four Horsemen—Conquest (riding a white horse), War (red horse), Famine (black horse with scales), and Death (pale horse). These riders emerge as the Lamb of God (Jesus Christ) breaks the first four of seven seals, symbolizing widespread destruction, societal collapse, and plagues preceding the Last Judgment.

The Four Riders

- The Rider on the White Horse:

    o Symbolism: Often interpreted as the Antichrist, or the spirit of conquest and deception.

    o Action: He rides out with a bow, bringing false peace or a new order that leads to greater destruction.

    o

129

- The Rider on the Red Horse:

    o Symbolism: Represents war, bloodshed, and conflict.

    o Action: This rider takes peace from the earth, equipped with a great sword to kill and bring about widespread violence.

- The Rider on the Black Horse:

    o Symbolism: Symbolizes famine and scarcity.

    o Action: He carries a pair of scales weighing a day's food supply, indicating high prices and a severe lack of food.

- The Rider on the Pale (or Green) Horse:

    o Symbolism: Represents death, plague, and devastation.

    o Action: His name is Death, and Hades follows close behind him, given authority over a fourth of the earth to kill by sword, famine, plague, and wild animals.

Context in the Book of Revelation

- The Seven Seals: The Four Horsemen are released when the Lamb of God opens the first four of seven seals on a scroll that God holds.

- Divine Judgment: Their appearance heralds a destructive period of judgment on the world, known as the Great Tribulation, and serves as a harbinger of the end times.

Russia's presence in Bible prophecy is most directly tied to the Gog of Magog prophecy in Ezekiel 38 and 39, where "Rosh," "Meshech," and "Tubal" are interpreted by some scholars to refer to regions of ancient and modern Russia. This prophecy describes a future leader from the land of Magog, identified as the "prince of Rosh," who will lead an invading coalition against Israel from the north, with nations like Persia (Iran) also involved.

Key Points

- Ezekiel 38-39 is the primary text linking Russia to biblical prophecy.

- Gog: The leader of the invading force is referred to as Gog.

- Land of Magog: The invading force originates from the land of Magog.

- Rosh, Meshech, and Tubal: The prince of these lands is a leader, with "Rosh" interpreted as a place name, or the leader of what corresponds to Russia.

- Geographical Context: Russia is situated to the north of Israel.

- Coalition: The prophecy involves an alliance of nations, including Russia, Iran (Persia), Libya, and Turkey.

- Timing: The prophecy is understood to refer to a future event that will occur when Israel is in relative safety.

- Outcome: God's judgment will fall upon the invading army.

- Divine Intervention: God will intervene to protect Israel.

Notes